The Gold Thread

Norman Macleod

CONTENTS

Dedication
To My Children

I dedicate this story to you, because it was for you I first wrote it, and to you I first read it among the green hills of Moffat. It was afterwards printed in Good Words, and now you see it again appears as a little book for other children, who, I hope, will like it as much as you do.

I wish to help and encourage you, and all who read this story, to learn the great lesson which it is intended to teach; that lesson is, that we should always trust God and do what is right, and thus hold fast our gold thread in spite of every temptation and danger, being certain that in this way only will God lead us in safety and peace to His home.

Now, God gives each of you this gold thread to hold fast in your own house or in school, in the nursery or in the play-ground, on every day and in every place. His voice in your heart, and in His Word, will also tell you always what is right, if you only listen to it. You, too, will be constantly tempted in some way or other to give up your gold thread, and to be selfish, disobedient, lazy, or untruthful. Many things, in short, will tempt you to do your own will rather than God's will.

You already know, and I hope you will always love and remember, those true stories in the Bible about the good men of the olden time, whose lives are there written. Now, what shewed that they were good? It was this, that they trusted God, and did what was right. If they ever let this their gold thread go, they lost their way and became unhappy; but when they held it fast, it led them in a way of peace and safety. To see how true this is, you have only to recall such stories as those of Noah, Abraham, Joseph, Moses, Job, Caleb and Joshua, Samuel, David and Jonathan, Elijah and Elisha, Hezekiah, Jeremiah, Daniel and his three companions, &c., &c., with those told you in the Book of Acts, not to mention the history of Jesus Christ, the perfect example for us all.

That you, my dear children, may be "followers of those who through faith and patience now inherit the promises," and thus be "followers of God as dear children," is the constant prayer of your mother, and of your father,

Norman Macleod

Norman Macleod

1. The Wanderer

Once upon a time, a boy lost his way in a vast forest that filled many a valley, and passed over many a hill, a rolling sea of leaves for miles and miles, further than the eye could reach. His name was Eric, son of the good King Magnus. He was dressed in a blue velvet dress, with a gold band round his waist, and his fair locks in silken curls waved from his beautiful head. But his hands and face were scratched, and his clothes torn with the briars, as he ran here and there like one much perplexed.

Sometimes he made his

way through tangled brushwood, or crossed the little grassy plains in the forest, now losing himself in dark ravines, then climbing up their steep sides, or crossing with difficulty the streams that hurried through them. For a long time he kept his heart up, and always said to himself,

"I shall find it, I shall find it;" until, as the day advanced, he was wearied and hungry; and every now and then he cried,

"Oh, my father! where is my father! I'm lost! I'm lost!"

Or, "Where, oh, where is my gold thread!"

All day the forest seemed to him to be very sad. He had never seen it so gloomy. There was a strange sadness in the rustle of the leaves, and a sadness in the noise of the streams. He did not hear the birds sing as they used to do. But he heard the ravens croak with their hoarse voice, as their black forms swept along the precipices which here and there rose above the trees. The large hawks, too, always appeared to be wheeling over his head, pausing, and fluttering as if about to dart down upon him.

Why was he so sad? Why was he so afraid?

But on Eric journeyed, in the hope of finding his way out of the boundless forest, or of meeting some one who would be his guide. At last, the sun appeared to be near its setting, and he could see the high branches of the trees, shining like gold, as its last rays fell upon them. But underneath, the foliage was getting darker and darker; the birds were preparing to sleep, and everything soon became so still that he could hear his steps echoing through the wood, and when he stopped, he heard his heart beating, or a leaf falling; but nowhere did he see a house, and no human being had he met since morning. Then the wind suddenly began to rise, and he heard it at first creeping along the tree-tops like a gentle whisper, and by and by to call louder and louder for the storm to come. Dark clouds gathered over the sky, and rushed along chased by the winds, that were soon to fight with the giant trees.

At last, he sat down at the root of a great old oak, burying his face in his hands, not knowing what to do. He then tried to climb the tree, in order to spend the night among its branches, in case wild beasts should attack him. But as he was climbing it, he heard some one singing with a loud voice. Listening attentively, and looking eagerly through the leaves, he saw a boy apparently older than himself, dressed in rough shaggy clothes, made from skins of wild animals. His long matted hair escaped over his cheeks from under a black bearskin cap. With a short thick stick he was driving a herd of swine through the wood. "Hey there, you black porker!" cried the boy, as he threw a stone at some pig which was running away. "Get along, you lazy long-snout!" he shouted to another, as he came thump on its back with his cudgel. And then he sung this song with a loud voice which made the woods ring:--

"Oh, there's nothing half so fine,
As to drive a herd of swine,
And through the forest toddle,
With nothing in my noddle,
 But rub-a-dub, rub-dub,
hey-up, halloo!

"When I wish to have some fun,
 Then I make the porkers run,
Till they gallop, snort, and wheeze,
Among the leafy trees;
Oh, rub-a-dub, rub-dub,
hey-up, halloo!

"How their backs begin to bristle,
When I shout aloud and whistle!
How they kick at every lick ,

That I give them with my stick!
Oh, rub-a-dub, rub-dub,
hey-up, halloo!"

"Get along, you rascals," cried the savage-looking herd, "or I'll kill and roast you before your time." But soon the herd, with his swine, were concealed from Eric's sight by the wood; though he still heard his "rub-a-dub" chorus, to which he beat time with a sort of rude drum, made with a dried skin and hoop. Eric determined to make his acquaintance, or at all events to follow him to some house; so he descended from the tree, and ran off in the direction from which he heard the song coming. He soon over-took him.

"Hollo!" said the wild-looking lad, with as much astonishment as if Eric had fallen from the clouds: "Who? where from? where to?"

"I have lost my way in the wood," said Eric, "and want you to guide me."

"To Ralph?" asked the swineherd. "Ralph! pray, who is he?"

"Master, chief, captain, everything, everybody," replied the young savage. "I will go anywhere for shelter, as night is coming on; but I will reward you if you bring me to my father's home."

"Who is your father, my fine fellow?" inquired the swineherd, leaning on his stick.

"The king," replied Eric.

"You lie, Sir Prince! Ralph is king."

"I speak the truth, swineherd."

The swineherd by this time was examining Eric's dress with an impudent look.

"Pay me now," said he; "give me this gold band, and I will guide you."

"I cannot give you this gold band, for my father gave it to me, and I have lost enough to-day. By the by, did you see a gold thread waving anywhere among the trees?"

"A gold thread! what do you mean? I saw nothing but pigs until I saw you, and I shall treat you like a pig, d'ye hear? and lick you too, for I have no time to put off. So give me your band. Come, be quick!" said he, with his fierce face, and holding up his stick as he came up to Eric.

"Keep off, swineherd; don't touch me!"

"Don't touch you! why shouldn't I touch you? Do you see this stick? How would you like to have it among your fine curls, as I drive it among the pigs' bristles?" And he began to flourish it over his head, and to press nearer and nearer. "Once, twice, when I say thrice, if you do not unbuckle, I shall save you the trouble, and leave you to the wild beasts, who would like a tender bit of prince's flesh better than pork. Come; once! twice!"

Eric was on his guard, and said, "I shall fight you, you young robber, till death, rather than give you this band,--so keep off."

"Thrice!" shouted the herd, and down came his thick cudgel, which he intended should fall on Eric's head. But Eric sprang aside, and before he could recover himself, dashed in upon him, tripped him up, and threw him on the grass, seizing him by the throat in a moment. The herd, in his efforts to get out of Eric's grasp, let go his cudgel, which Eric seized, and held over his head.

"Unless you promise, Master Swineherd, to leave me alone, I may leave you alone with the wild beasts." "You are stronger than I thought," said the herd. "Let me up, or I shall be choked. Let me up, I say, and I promise to guide you."

"I shall trust you," said Eric, "though you would not trust me. Rise!"

So the herd rose, and picked up his cap, but Eric would not give him his stick until he guided him to some house.

"Come along," said he, sulkily.

"What is your name?" asked Eric.

"They call me Wolf. I killed a wolf once with my boar-spear."

"Why, Wolf, did you try to kill me?"

"Because I wanted your gold belt."

"But it is a great sin to rob and kill."

"Other people rob me, and would kill me too, if I did not take care of their pigs," said Wolf, carelessly.

"You should fear God, Wolf."

"I fear that name truly, for Ralph always swears by it when he is in a rage. But I do not know what it means."

"Oh, Wolf, surely your father and mother told you about God, who made all things, and made you and me; God, who loves us, and wishes us to love Him, and to do what is right?"

"I have no father or mother," replied Wolf, "nor brothers or sisters, and I do not know God. No one cares for me but my pigs, and so I sleep with them, and eat with them."

"Poor fellow!" said Eric with a look of kindness, "I am sorry for you. Here is all the money I have. Take it. I wish to shew you that I have no ill-will to you;" and Eric gave him a gold coin.

Wolf gave a grunt like one of his pigs, and began his song of "Rub-a-dub." "No one ever gave me money before," remarked Wolf almost to himself, as he examined the coin on his rough hand, which looked like tanned leather. "How much is this?" inquired Wolf. Eric explained its value. The herd was astonished, and began to think what he could purchase with it. "It would buy a large pig," he said.

He seemed very anxious to conceal the coin, and so he hid it in the top of his hairy cap.

"See that tall tower," said Wolf, "which looks like a rock above the trees; that is the only house near for twenty miles round. You can reach it soon; and when you do reach it," said Wolf, speaking low, as if some one might hear him, "take my advice, and get away as fast as you can from my master Ralph, for"--and Wolf gave a number of winks, as much as to say, I know something.

"What do you mean?" asked Eric. "Oh, nothing, nothing; but take Wolf's advice, and say to Ralph you are a beggar. Put the gold band in your pocket, and swear to remain with him, but run off when you can. Cheat him; that's my way."

"It is not my way," replied Eric, "and, come what may, never can be, for a voice says to me,

"'Better to die Than ever to lie.'"

"Ha! ha!" said Wolf; "I wish you lived with Ralph. He would teach you another lesson, my lad."

"I would rather that I had you, Wolf, to live in my house. I would be kind to you, and help you to be good, and tell you about God, who lives in the sky."

"And is that He who is speaking? Listen!" Thunder began to mutter in the clouds. "Yes, it is He," replied Eric; "and if you will only listen, you can also hear Him often speak with a small, still voice in your heart."

"I never heard Him," replied Wolf; "but I cannot stay longer with you, for my pigs will wander: there is a black rascal who always leads them astray. Now, king's son, give Wolf the stick; it is all he has."

"Here it is to you, and I am sure you will not use it wrongly; you will try and be good, Wolf? for it will make you happy."

"Humph," said Wolf, "I am happy when I get my pigs home, and Ralph does not strike me. But I must away, and see you don't tell any one you gave me money. They would rob me." And away he ran among the trees in search of his pigs, while Eric heard his little drum, and his song of "Rub-a-dub, halloo!" die away in the distance. Another loud peal and flash of lightning made Eric start, and off he ran towards a light which now beamed from the tower. But he thought to himself, "I am much worse than that poor Wolf, for I knew what was right, and did not do it. I heard the voice, but did not attend to it. Oh, my father, why did I not obey you!"

2. The Robbers Tower

Sometimes he lost sight of the light, and again he caught it, till it became brighter and brighter, and very soon he came to a high rock, on the top of which was perched a tall, dark tower. After groping about, he found a narrow path that led up to the tower, from one of the windows of which the light was brightly shining. He ascended a flight of steep steps till he reached a massive door covered with iron. He knocked as loud as he could, when a large dog began barking furiously inside, and springing up to the door, as if it would tear it down.

Then a gruff voice called out of a window over the door, "Who is there? Who disturbs me in this way?"

The little boy replied, "Please, sir, I am Eric, son of King Magnus, and I have lost my way in this wood."

"The son of the king, are you?" asked the voice. "That is a grand joke! Let me have a sight of you." Then the window was shut, and he heard footsteps coming tramp, tramp, down the stairs, and the voice said to the dog, "Lie down, hound, and don't be greedy! You would not eat a young prince, would you? Lie down, Tuscar!" The door was then opened by a fierce-looking man, with a long beard. The man bid him enter, and examined him about himself and his journey. Eric answered truly every question. Then the man rang a bell for an old woman who lived in the house, and bid her take the boy with her, and give him his supper.

The old woman looked very ugly and very cross, and led him up, up, a great number of dark, gloomy stairs, until she reached a small room, with a bed and table in it, where she bade Eric wait till she brought him supper. The big hound followed them, and stayed in the room while the woman went away. Eric was at first afraid of the dog, he was so large and wild-looking, but he came and laid his head on his knee, and he scratched his ears, and patted him, and was very kind to him. The supper came, and the boy managed to keep a few bits of meat out of his own supper for the dog, and when the old woman went out of the room, he fed the hound, who seemed very hungry, and said to him,

"Tuscar, old fellow, I like you very much. Take another bit, good dog, and be happy!" The dog wagged his tail, and looked up kindly with his large eyes, for he was thankful for his supper, and ate much more than Eric.

"Now," said the old woman gruffly, when she took away the remains of the supper, "you have ate what would do me for a week. You won't starve, Master Prince. Go to bed." The old woman left him, but suddenly returning, she discovered Eric on his knees. As he rose, she scoffed and jeered him, and asked,

"Do you always say your prayers?"

"Yes, always," replied the boy. "Who taught you?"

"My mother, who is dead." The old woman

heaved a deep sigh, but the boy did not know why. Perhaps she used to pray when she was a little girl herself, and had given up speaking to God, or even thinking of Him, and so had become wicked; or perhaps she thought of some child of her own whom she had never taught to pray. She soon went away without speaking a word more, and Eric was left in darkness. He looked out through the narrow window of his room, but could see nothing but black clouds rushing over the sky. Far down he heard a stream roaring, and the wind, which now blew a gale, came booming over the tree-tops, and howling round the tower. Every now and then a flash lighted up the forest, and the thunder crashed in the sky. It was a fearful night!

Some time after, he heard footsteps at his door, and immediately the man with the beard entered, and sat down. "Do you know," he asked, "where your father is?"

"No," said Eric; "as I told you, I lost my way in the forest, and have been wandering all day, and cannot find him; but perhaps you will send some one to-morrow with me to shew me the way to his castle, and I am sure my kind, good father will give you a rich reward."

"You are very, very far from your father's house,"

said the man, "and I fear you will never see him again; but come with me, and I shall shew you some beautiful things that will please you." So the man took Eric by the hand, and, carrying a lamp, he led him into a room that seemed full of gold and silver, with beautiful dresses, sparkling with diamonds, and every kind of splendour, and he said,

"Stay with me, my boy, and I will give you all this, for I am a king too, and will make you my heir."

"Oh, no, no," said Eric; "I will never forsake my own father."

The man then said, "If you stay with me, you need never go to school all day, but may amuse yourself from morning till night, and have a beautiful pony to ride, and a gun to shoot deer with, and also fishing-rods, and a servant to attend you, and any kind of meat and drink you like best. Do stay with me!"

"You are very kind," said Eric, "but I cannot be happy without my father."

"Come then with me, my fine fellow, and I shall shew you something different," said the man, seizing Eric firmly by the arm, and looking very angry. After walking along a passage, from the end of which confused noises came, a door was opened, and in a large hall, round a great oak table, sat a company of fierce-looking men, drinking from large flagons which stood before them. Their faces were red, and their eyes gleamed like fire. Ralph placed Eric on the table.

One of the robbers was singing this song:--
"We're the famous robber band-- Hurrah!
The lords of all the land-- Hurrah!
A fig for law or duty,
If we only get our booty;
With a fa, lal, la, la, la!

"'Every man to mind himself,'
Hurrah! Is the rule of Captain Ralph!
Hurrah! Then let the greatest thief
And robber be our chief--
With a fa, lal, la, la, la!"

No wonder poor Eric trembled as he heard that lawless band thus glorying in their shame, and like demons singing their horrid song in praise of all that was most dreadful and most wicked. He had read stories of robbers, which sometimes made him think that they were fine, brave fellows; but now that he was among them, he saw how depraved, cruel, and frightful they were. Their savage, coarse looks terrified him; but he was held by Ralph on the table. When the song was ended, one of them asked,

"Whom have we got here?"

"Who do you think?" replied Ralph. "What would you say, my men, to a young prince,--no less than the son of our great enemy, King Magnus?"

"A young prince! The son of Magnus! What a prize!" they exclaimed. "What shall we do with him?"

"First of all, let us have his gold belt," said Ralph, unbuckling Eric's belt.

"Ha! what a pretty thing it is!"

"My father gave it to me, and I don't wish to part with it. The swineherd Wolf tried to take it from me, but I fought him, and kept it," said Eric.

"Wolf is a brave young robber," replied Ralph, "and he shall have it for his trouble. In the meantime, my lad, it is mine. But what, my men, shall we do with the prince?"

Kill him," said one.

"Starve him to death," said another.

"Put his eyes out, and send him back to his father," said a third.

Eric prayed to God, but said nothing.

"I propose," said Ralph, "to make him a captain if he will stay with us."

"Never!" said Eric; "I would rather die!"

"Let him die, then," said a fierce robber; "for his father hung my brother for killing one of his nobles."

"I tell you what we will do with the lion's whelp," said Ralph; "let us keep him in prison, and send a message to his father, that we have him snug in a den among the mountains, and that, unless he sends us an immense ransom, we shall kill him."

"That will do famously," said the robbers; "so off with him!" Then Ralph led the boy down stairs,--

down, down, until he thought they never would stop, and at last they came to an iron door, with great bars on it, and a large lock, and he turned to Eric, and said, "I know your father, and I hate him! for he sends his soldiers after me, and tries to save travellers from me, and now I have got his son. I will keep you here till you die, or till he pays!" Then he opened the dungeon door, and thrust Eric in. When it closed, it echoed like thunder through the passages. Eric cast himself down on the dungeon floor.

All appeared to be a strange dream. Oh, how he repented having disobeyed his father! and how he seemed to be as bad as the dreadful robbers in having done what he pleased, and followed his own will, instead of doing what was right! About an hour after, he heard some rustling, as if high up on the wall, and a voice whispered

"Eric!"

"Who is there?" asked Eric, and his little heart trembled.

"Silence! quiet! it is Wolf. Here is a small window in your prison, and I have opened it outside; climb up, get out, and run for your life."

Eric heard no more, but scrambled in the dark up the rough stones in the wall until he reached the window, where he looked out, and saw the stars and the woods. He soon forced his way through, and dropped down on the opposite side. Some one caught him in his arms. It was Wolf.

"Here is your gold band, Eric. I got it from Ralph; for He who was speaking in the thunder has been saying things in my heart. You were kind to poor Wolf. Now escape! Fly! I shall close the window again. Ralph will never know how you got out, and he will not open the prison-door till after breakfast. So you have a long time. Run as long as you can along that road till you reach a hill, then cross it, until you reach a stream, which you must follow downwards. The worst of the storm is over, and the night will soon be calm. Off!"

"Bless you, Wolf!" said Eric; "I shall never forget you."

Poor Eric! how he ran, and ran, beneath the stars! He felt no fatigue for a time. He thought he heard the robbers after him; every time the wind blew loud, he imagined it was their wild cry. On he ran till he reached the hill, and crossed it, and came to a green spot beneath a rock, on the banks of the stream, when he could run no more, but fell down, and whether he fainted or fell asleep he could not tell.

Norman Macleod

3. The Journey Home

Eric knew not how long he slept, but, as
in a dream, he heard a sweet voice singing
these words:--

"Rest thee, boy, rest thee, boy, lonely and dreary,
Thy little heart breaking from losing the way;
Thy father has not left thee friendless, though weary,
When learning through suffering to fear and obey."

Eric opened his eyes, but moved not a limb,
as if under some strange fascination. It was
early morning. High over head a lark was
"singing like an angel in the clouds."
The mysterious voice went on in the same
beautiful and soothing strain—

"Oh, sweet is the lark as she sings o'er her nest,
And warbles unseen in the clear morning light;
But sweeter by far is the song in the breast
When in life's early morning we do what is right!"

Eric could neither move nor speak; but in his heart he confessed with sorrow that he had done what was wrong. And again the voice sang--

"Now, darling, awaken, thou art not forsaken! The old night is past and a new day begun; Let thy journey with love to thy father be taken, And at evening thy father will welcome thee home."

"I will arise and go to my father!" said Eric, springing to his feet. He saw beside him a beautiful lady, who looked like a picture he once saw of his mother, or like one of those angels from heaven about whom he had often read. And the lady said,

"Fear not! I know you, Eric, and how it came to pass that you are here. Your father sent you for a wise and good purpose through the forest, and gave you hold of a gold thread to guide you, and told you never to let it go. It was your duty to him to have held it fast; but instead of doing your duty, trusting and obeying your father, and keeping hold of the thread, you let it go to chase butterflies, and gather wild-berries, and to amuse yourself. This you did more than once. You neglected your father's counsels and warnings, and because of your self-confidence and self-pleasing, you lost your thread, and then you lost your way. What dangers and troubles have you thus got into through disobedience to your father's commands, and want of trust in his love and wisdom! For had you only followed your father's directions, the gold thread would have brought you to his beautiful castle, where there is to be a happy meeting of your friends, with all your brothers and sisters."

Poor little Eric began to weep!

"Listen to me, child," said the lady, kindly, "for you cannot have peace but by doing what is right. Know, then, that all your brothers and sisters made this very journey by help of the gold thread, and they are at home with great joy."

"Oh, save me! save me!" cried Eric, and caught the lady's hand.

"Yes, I will save you," said she, "if you will learn obedience. I know and love you, dear boy. I know and love your father, and have been sent by him to deliver you. I heard what you said, and know all you did, last night, and I was very glad that you proved, in trial, your love to your father, your love of truth, and your love of others, and this makes me hope all good of you for the future. Come now with me!"

And so the beautiful woman took him by the hand. The storm had passed away, and the sun was shining on the green leaves of the trees, and every drop of dew sparkled like a diamond. The birds were all warbling their morning hymns, and feeding their young ones in their nests. The streams were dancing down the rocks and through the glens. "The mountains broke forth into singing, and all the trees clapped their hands with joy." Everything thus seemed beautiful and happy to Eric, for he himself was happy at the thought of doing what was right, and of going home. The lady led him to a sunny glade in the wood, covered with wild flowers, from which the bees were busy gathering their honey, and she said,

"Now, child, are you willing to do your father's will?"

"Oh, yes!" "Will you do it, whatever dangers may

await you?"

"Yes!" "Well, then, I must tell you that your father has given me the gold thread which you lost; and he bids me again tell you, with his warm love, that if you keep hold of it, and follow it wherever it leads, you are sure to come to him at sunset; but if you let it go, you may wander on in this dark forest till you die, or are again taken prisoner by robbers. Know, also, that there is no other possible way of saving you, but by your following the gold thread."

"I am resolved to do my duty, come what may," said Eric. "May you be helped to do it!" said the lady. She then gave him a cake, to support him in his journey.

"And now, child," she added, "one advice more I will give you, and it was given you by your father, though you forgot it; it is this--if ever you feel the thread slipping from your hands, or are yourself tempted to let it go, pray immediately, and you will get wisdom and strength to find it, to lay hold of it, and to follow it. Before we part, kneel down and ask assistance to be good and obedient, brave and patient, until you meet your father." The little boy knelt down and repeated the Lord's Prayer; and as he said, "Thy will be done on earth, as it is done in heaven," he felt calm and happy as he used to do when he knelt at his mother's knee, and he thought her hand was waving over him, as if to bless him. When he lifted up his head there was no one there but himself; but he saw an old gray cross, and a gold thread was tied to it, and passed away, away, shining through the woods.

With a firm hold of his gold thread, the boy began his journey home. He passed along path-ways on which the brown leaves of last year's growth were thickly strewn, and from among which flowers of every colour were springing. He crossed little brooks that ran like silver threads, and tinkled like silver bells. He passed under trees with great trunks, and huge branches that swept down to the ground, and waved far up in the blue sky. The birds hopped about him, and looked down upon him from among the green leaves, and they sang him songs, and some of them seemed to speak to him. He thought one large bird like a crow cried, "Good boy! good boy!" and another whistled, "Cheer up! cheer up!" and so he went merrily on, and very often he gave the robins and blackbirds that came near him bits of his cake. After awhile, he came to a green spot in the middle of the wood, without trees, and a footpath went direct across it, to the place where the gold thread was leading him, and there he saw a sight that made him wonder and pause.

It was a bird about the size of a pigeon, with feathers like gold and a crown like silver, and it was slowly walking near him, and he saw gold eggs glittering in a nest among the grass a few yards off. Now, he thought, it would be such a nice thing to bring home a nest with gold eggs! The bird did not seem afraid of him, but stopped and looked at him with a calm blue eye, as if she said, "Surely you would not rob me?" He could not, however, reach the nest with his hand, and though he pulled and pulled the thread, it would not yield one inch, but seemed as stiff as a wire.

"I see the thread quite plain," said the boy to himself, "and the very place where it enters the dark wood on the other side. I will just leap to the nest, and in a moment I shall have the eggs in my pocket, and then spring back and catch the thread again. I cannot lose it here, with the sun shining; and, besides, I see it a long way before me." So he took one step to seize the eggs; but he was in such haste that he fell and crushed the nest, breaking the eggs to pieces, and the little bird screamed and flew away, and then suddenly the birds in the trees began to fly about, and a large owl swept out of a dark glade, and cried, "Whoo--whoo--whoo-oo-oo;" and a cloud came over the sun! Eric's heart beat quick, and he made a grasp at his gold thread, but it was not there! Another, and another grasp, but it was not there! and soon he saw it waving far above his head, like a gossamer thread in the breeze. You would have pitied him, while you could not have helped being angry with him for having been so silly and disobedient when thus tried, had you only seen his pale face, as he looked above him for his thread, and about him for the road, but could see neither! And he became so confused with his fall, that he did not know which side of the open glade he had entered, nor to which point he was travelling.

But at last he thought he heard a bird chirping, "Seek--seek--seek!" and another repeating, "Try again--try again--try--try!" and then he remembered what the lady had said to him, and he fell on his knees and told all his grief, and cried,

"Oh, give me back my thread! and help me never, never, to let it go again!"

As he lifted up his eyes, he saw the thread come slowly, slowly down; and when it came near, he sprang to it and caught it, and he did not know whether to laugh, or cry, or sing, he was so thankful and happy!

"Ah!" said he, "I hope I shall never forget this fall!"

That part of the Lord's Prayer came into his mind which says, "Lead us not into temptation, but deliver us from evil."

"Who would have thought," said he to himself, "that I was in any danger in such a beautiful, green, sunny place as this, and so very early, too, in my journey! Oh! shame upon me!"

As he proceeded with much more thought and caution, a large crow up a tree was hoarsely croaking, and seemed to say,

"Beware, beware!"

"Thank you, Mr Crow," said the boy, "I shall;" and he threw him a bit of bread for his good advice. But now the thread led him through the strangest places. One was a very dark, deep ravine, with a stream that roared and rushed far down, and overhead the rocks seemed to meet, and thick bushes concealed the light, and nothing could Eric see but the gold thread, that looked like a thread of fire, though even that grew dim sometimes, until he could only feel it in his hand. And whither he was going he knew not. At one time he seemed to be on the edge of a precipice, until it seemed as if the next step must lead him over, and plunge him down; but when he came to the very edge, the thread led him quite safely along it. At another, a rock which looked like a wall rose before him, and he said to himself, "Well, I must be stopped here! I shall never be able to climb up!" But just as he touched it, he found steps cut in it, and up, up, the thread guided him to the top! Then it would bring him down, down, until he once stood beside a raging stream, and the water foamed and dashed. "Now," he thought, "I must be drowned; but come what may, I will not let my thread go." And so it was, that when he came so near the stream as to feel the spray upon his cheek, and was sure that he must leap in if he followed his thread, what did he see but a little bridge that passed from bank to bank, and by which he crossed in perfect safety; until at last he began to lose fear, and to believe more and more that he would always be in the right road, so long as he did not trust mere appearances, but kept hold of his thread!

Norman Macleod

4. The Great Lion

But Eric had now to endure a great
trial of his faith in the thread. As he
journeyed on, it led him up a winding path
towards the summit of a hill. The large trees
of the forest were soon left behind, and small
stunted bushes grew among masses of gray rocks.
The path was like the bed of a dry brook, and was
often very steep. There were no birds except little
stone-chats, that hopped and chirped among the
large round stones. Far below, he could see the tops
of the trees, and here and there a stream glittering
under the sunbeams. Nothing disturbed the silence
but the hoarse croak of the raven, or the wild cry of
a kite or eagle, that, like a speck, wheeled far up in
the sky. But suddenly, Eric heard a roar like thunder
coming from the direction towards which the
thread was leading him. He stopped for a moment,
but the thread was firm in his hand, and led right up
the hill. On he went, and no wonder he started,
when, as he turned the corner of a rock, he heard

another roar, and saw the head of a huge lion looking out of what seemed to be a cave, a few yards back from the edge of a dizzy precipice! He saw, too, that the path he must follow was between the lion's den and the precipice. What now was to be done? Should he give up his thread and fly? No! A voice in his heart encouraged him to be brave and not fear, and he knew from his experience that he had always been led in safety and peace when he followed the road, holding fast to his thread. He was certain that his father never would deceive him, or bid him do anything but what was right; and he was sure, too, that the lady, from her love to him, and her teaching him to trust God and to pray, would not have bid him do anything that was wrong. And then an old verse his father taught him came into his mind--

"In the darkest night, my child,
Canst thou see the Right, my child?
Forward then! God is near!
The Right will be light to thee,
Armour and might to thee;
Forward! and never fear!"

So Eric resolved to go on in faith. There was just one thing he saw which cheered him, and that was a white hare, sitting with her ears cocked, quite close to the lion's den, and he wondered how she had no fear, but he could not explain it at the time. On he walked, but he could hardly breathe, as the thread led still nearer and nearer to the den. These big eyes were glaring on him, and seemed to draw him closer and closer! There the lion stood, on one side of the path, while the great precipice descended on the other. One step more, and he was between these two dangers. He moved on until he was so near that he seemed to feel the lion's breath, and then the brute sprang out on him, and tried to strike him with his huge paw that would have crushed him to the dust! Eric shut his eyes, and gave himself up for lost. But the lion suddenly fell back, for he was held fast by a great iron chain, and so Eric passed in safety!

Oh, how thankful he was! and how gladly he ran down hill, the lion in his den roaring behind him! Down he ran until all was quiet again. As he pursued his journey in the beautiful green woods, something told him his greatest trial was past. He felt very peaceful and strong. And now, as he reached some noble old beech-trees, the thread fell on the grass, and he took this as a sign that he should lie down too, and so he did, grateful for the rest. He ate some of his cake, and drank from a clear spring beside him, and feasted on wild strawberries which grew in abundance all round him. He then stretched himself on his back among soft moss, and looked up through the branches of the gigantic tree, and saw with delight the sunlight speckling the emerald green leaves and brown bark with touches of silver, and, far up, the deep blue sky with white clouds reposing on it, like snowy islands on a blue ocean; and he watched the squirrels, with their bushy tails, as they ran up the tree, and jumped from branch to branch, and sported among the leaves, until he fell into a sort of pleasant day-dream, and felt so happy, he hardly knew why. As he lay here, he thought he heard, in his half-waking dream, a little squirrel sing a song. Was it not his own heart, now so glad because doing what was right, which was singing? This was the song which he thought he heard:--

"I'm a merry, merry squirrel,
 All day I leap and whirl,
Through my home in the old beech-tree;
If you chase me, I will run
 In the shade and in the sun,
But you never, never can catch me!
For round a bough I'll creep,
Playing hide-and-seek so sly,

Or through the leaves bo-peep,
 With my little shining eye.
Ha, ha, ha! ha, ha, ha! ha, ha, ha!

"Up and down I run and frisk,
 With my bushy tail to whisk
All who mope in the old beech-trees;
How droll to see the owl,
As I make him wink and scowl,
When his sleepy, sleepy head I tease!
And I waken up the bat,
Who flies off with a scream,
For he thinks that I'm the cat
Pouncing on him in his dream.
Ha, ha, ha! ha, ha, ha! ha, ha, ha!

"Through all the summer long
 I never want a song,
From my birds in the old beech-trees;
I have singers all the night,
And, with the morning bright,
Come my busy humming fat brown bees.
When I've nothing else to do,
With the nursing birds I sit,
And we laugh at the cuckoo
A-cuckooing to her tit!
Ha, ha, ha! ha, ha, ha! ha, ha, ha!

"When winter comes with snow,
And its cruel tempests blow
All the leaves from my old beech-trees;
Then beside the wren and mouse
I furnish up a house,
Where like a prince I live at my ease!
 What care I for hail or sleet,
With my hairy cap and coat;
And my tail across my feet,
Or wrapp'd about my throat!
Ha, ha, ha! ha, ha, ha! ha, ha, ha!"

As Eric opened his eyes, and looked up, he saw a little squirrel with its tail curling up its back, sitting on a branch looking down upon him; and then it playfully ran away with the tail down and waving after it.

"Farewell, happy little fellow!" said Eric; "I must do my work now, and play like you afterwards;" for at that moment the thread again became tight, and Eric, refreshed with his rest, and hearty for his journey, stepped out bravely. He saw, at some distance, and beyond an open glade in the forest, a rapid river towards which he was descending. When near the river, he perceived something struggling in the water, and then heard a loud cry or scream for help, as if from one drowning. He was almost tempted to run off to his assistance without his thread, but he felt thankful that the thread itself led in the very direction from whence he heard the cries coming.

So off he ran as fast as he could, and as he came to the brink of a deep, dark pool in the river, he saw the head of a boy rising above the water, as the poor little fellow tried to keep himself afloat. Now he sank--again he rose--until he suddenly disappeared. Eric laid hold of his thread with a firm hand, and leaped in over head and ears, and then rose to the surface, and with his other hand swam to where the boy had sank. He soon caught him, and brought him with great difficulty to the surface, which he never could have done unless the thread had supported them both above the water.

"Eric!" cried the gasping boy, opening his eyes, almost covered by his long, wet hair.

"Wolf!" cried Eric, "is it you?"

It was indeed poor Wolf, who lay panting on the dry land, with his rough garments dripping with water, and himself hardly able to move.

"Oh, tell me, Wolf, what brought you here! I am so glad to have helped you!" After a little time, when Wolf could speak, he told him in his own way, bit by bit, how Ralph had suspected him; and how the old woman had heard him speaking as she was looking out of an upper window; and how when Ralph asked the gold belt he could not give it; and how he was obliged himself to fly; and how he had been running for his life for hours.

"Now let us fly," said Wolf; "I am quite strong again. I fear that they are in pursuit of us."

They both went on at a quick pace, Eric having shewn Wolf the wonderful thread, and explained to him how he must never part with it, come what may, and having also given him a bit of his cake to comfort him.

"O rub-a-dub, dub!" said Wolf, squeezing the water out of his hair, as he trotted along; "I am glad to be away. Ralph would have killed me like a pig. The voice told me to run after you."

So on they went together, happy again to meet. Suddenly Wolf stopped, and listening with anxious face, he said,

"Hark! did you hear anything?"

"No," said Eric, "what was it?"

"Hush!--listen!--there again--I hear it!"

"I think I do hear something far off like a dog's bark," replied Eric. "Hark!" So they both stopped and listened, and far away they heard a deep

"Bow-wow-wow-wow-o-o-o-o-o" echoing through the forest.

"Let us run as fast as we can," said the boy, in evident fear; "hear him!--hear him!"

"Bow-wow-wow-o-o-o-o," and the sound came nearer and nearer.

"What is it? why are you so afraid?" inquired Eric.

"Oh! that is Ralph's bloodhound, Tuscar," cried Wolf, "and he is following us. He won't perhaps touch me, but you he may." So Eric ran as fast as he could, but never let go the gold thread, which this time led towards a steep hill, which they were obliged to scramble up.

"Run, Eric!--quick--hide--up a tree--anywhere!"

"I cannot, I dare not," said Eric; "whatever happens, I must hold fast my thread."

But they heard the "Bow-wow-o-o-o" coming nearer and nearer, and as they looked back they saw the large hound rush out of the wood, and as he came to the water, catching sight of the boys on the opposite hill, he leaped in, and in a few minutes would be near them. And now he came bellowing like a fierce bull up the hill, his tongue hanging out, and his nose tracking along the ground, as he followed their footsteps.

"I shall run and meet him," said Wolf, "and stop him if I can;" and down ran the swineherd, calling,

"Tuscar! Tuscar! good dog, Tuscar!" Tuscar knew Wolf, and passed him, but ran up to Eric. As he reached Eric, who stood calm and firm, the bloodhound stopped, panting, smelling his clothes all round, but, strange to say, wagging his huge tail! He then ran back the way he had come, as if he had made a mistake, and all his race was for nothing! How was this? Ah, poor Tuscar remembered the supper Eric had given him, and was grateful for his kindness!

Wolf was astonished at Eric's escape, until he heard how he and Tuscar had become acquainted; and then Wolf heard the voice in his heart say that there was nothing better than kindness and love shewn to man or beast. They both after this pursued their journey with light and hopeful hearts, for they had got out of what was called the wild robber country, and Eric knew that he was drawing near home. The thread was stronger than ever, and every hour it helped more and more to support him. Wolf trotted along with his short stick, and sometimes snorting and blowing with the fatigue like one of his own pigs. They talked as best they could about all they had seen.

"Did you see big Thorold the lion?" asked Wolf.

"I did," said Eric; "he is very awful, but he was chained."

"Lucky for you!" said Wolf, "for Ralph hunts with him and kills travellers. He will obey none but Ralph. I heard him roaring. He is hungry. He once ate one of my pigs, and would have ate me if he had not first caught the poor black porker. I escaped up a tree."

And thus they chatted, as they journeyed on through woods, and across green plains, and over low hills, until Wolf complained of hunger. Eric at once gave him what remained of his large cake; but it did not suffice to appease the hunger of the herd, who was, however, very thankful for what he got.

To their delight they now saw a beautiful cottage not far from their path, and, as they approached it, an old woman, with a pretty girl who seemed to be her daughter, came out to meet them.

"Good day, young gentlemen!" said the old woman with a kind smile and a courtesy; "you seem to be on your travels, and look wearied? Pray come into my cottage, and I shall refresh you."

"What fortunate fellows we are!" said Wolf.

"We are much obliged to you for your hospitality," replied Eric. But, alas! the thread drew him in an opposite direction; so turning to Wolf, he said, "I cannot go in."

"Come, my handsome young gentleman," said the young woman, "and we shall make you so happy. You shall have such a dinner as will delight you, I am sure; and you may remain as long as you please, and I will dance and sing to you; nor need you pay anything." And she came forward smiling and dancing, offering her arm to Eric. "Surely you won't be so rude as refuse me! you are so beautiful, and have such lovely hair and eyes, and I never saw such a belt as you wear: do come!"

"Come, my son," said the old woman to Wolf, as she put her hand round his neck.

"With all my heart!" replied Wolf; "for, to tell the truth, I am wearied and hungry; one does not get such offers as yours every day."

"I cannot go," again said Eric. They could not see the thread, for to some it was invisible; but he saw it, and felt it like a wire passing away from the cottage.

"Who are you, kind friends?" inquired Eric.

"Friends of the king and of his family. Honest subjects, good people," said the old woman.

"Do you know Prince Eric?" asked Wolf.

"Right well!" replied the young woman. "He is a great friend of mine; a fine, tall, comely youth. He calls me his own little sweetheart."

"It is false!" said Eric; "you do not know him. You should not lie." But he did not tell her who he was, neither did Wolf, for Eric had made a sign to him to be silent.

"I won't enter your dwelling," said Eric, "for my duty calls me away."

They both gave a loud laugh, and said,

"Hear him! Only hear a fine young fellow talking about duty! Pleasure, ease, and liberty are for the young. We only want to make you happy: come!"

"I shall go with you," said Wolf; "do come, Eric."

"Wolf, speak to me," whispered Eric to the swineherd. "You know I cannot go, for my duty tells me to follow the thread. But now I see that this is the house of the wicked, for you heard how they lied; they neither know the king nor his children; and they laugh too at duty. Be advised, Wolf, and follow me."

Wolf hesitated, and looked displeased.

"Only for an hour, Eric!"

"Not a minute. Wolf. If you trust them more than me, go; but I am sure you and I shall never meet again."

"Then I will trust you, Eric," said Wolf; "the voice in my heart tells me to do so."

And so they both passed on. But the old woman and the girl began to abuse them, and call them all manner of evil names, and to laugh at them as silly fellows. The girl threw stones at them, which made Wolf turn round and flourish his stick over his head. At last they entered the cottage, the old woman shaking her fist, and calling out from the door,

"I'll soon send my friend Ralph after you!"

"Oh, ho! is that the way the wind blows!" exclaimed Wolf, with a whistle; and, grasping Eric's arm, said,

"You were right, prince! I never suspected them. I see now they are bad."

"I saw that before," replied Eric, "and knew that no good would come to us from making their acquaintance."

"Were they not cunning?"

"Yes; but, probably, with all their smiles, flattery, and fair promises, they would have proved more cruel in the end than either Ralph or old Thorold."

"What would they have done to us? Why did they meet us? Who are they, think you?"

"I don't know, Wolf; it was enough for me that they lied, and did not wish us to do what was right. The gold thread given me by my father never could have led me into the society and house of the wicked. I am glad we held it fast."

The Gold Thread (Illustrated)

5. Green Island of the Lake

Not long after this strange adventure, they reached a rising ground, from which a magnificent view burst upon them. Below, there was a large lake, surrounded by wooded hills, above which rose noble rocks fringed with stately pines, and higher ranges of mountains beyond, some of whose summits were covered with snow that glittered like purest alabaster in the azure blue of the sky. Eric gave a cry of joy; for he saw the house of one of his father's foresters, which he had once visited with his father.

"Wolf! Wolf!" he exclaimed, "look yonder, that is the house of Darkeye, the forester. We are safe!"

And the thread was leading straight down in the very direction which they wished. Darkeye's house was built on a small green island in the lake.

The island was like a little fort, for on every side the rocks descended like a wall. It could only be approached by a boat, which Darkeye kept on the island, and then by a narrow stair cut out of the rock at the landing-place. No robbers could thus get near it, and Darkeye was there to give shelter to travellers, and to help any of the poor who had to pass that way.

The thread led down to the shore. They forgot their fatigue, and ran down till they reached the ferry.

"Boat, ahoy!" shouted Eric. By and by two boys were seen running out of the cottage, and after looking cautiously at those who were calling for the boat, they rowed off, and soon were at the shore, where stood Eric with his gold belt, and Wolf in his rough skins.

"Olaf! Torquil! don't you remember me?" asked Eric, looking at his old friends. The boys looked astonished as they recognised the young prince, and received him joyfully into their boat, he holding by the thread, which seemed to cross the ferry towards the cottage. How many questions were mutually put and answered in a few minutes! They told him their father was at home; and how he had lately seen the king; and how the king was anxiously looking for

Eric's return; and how glad all on the island would be to see him; and the younger boy, Torquil, told him how they had now a tame otter, that fished in the lake, and a fine golden eagle which they had got young in her nest, that also lived on the island with them; and how their mother had got another baby since he had been there, and how happy they all were, and so on, until they arrived at the island, and there was old Darkeye himself waiting to receive them; and when he saw who was in the boat, he ran down the stone steps and grasped the young prince's hand, and drew him to his heart.

"Welcome! welcome!" said he; "I knew you had been in the forest, but your father would not tell me anything more about you. He only said that he longed for your coming home. But who is this?" asked Darkeye, pointing to Wolf.

"A friend of mine," said Eric, with a smile.

"My name is Wolf," grunted the swineherd.

"I think I have seen him before. But no! What? Yes!" said Darkeye, examining him; then added, as if he had discovered some old acquaintance, "Surely I have seen him. Tell me, my fine fellow, did you"--- - It was evident Darkeye had seen Wolf killing his game, or in some affray with the robbers. Wolf looked sternly at Darkeye, then at Eric, but said nothing.

"Oh, Darkeye, do not trouble poor Wolf," said Eric, "but let him go into the cottage; and come you with me, as I wish to tell you all that has happened to me during these few days."

So, while the boys took Wolf to the cottage, and food was being prepared, Eric told Darkeye all his adventures; and you would have been sure that the forester was hearing something which surprised and interested him wonderfully, had you seen his face, and how he sometimes laughed, or knit his brows and looked angry, or sad and solemn, or sprung to his feet from the rock on which he was sitting beside Eric. When Eric came to speak about the old woman and her daughter,

"Ah!" said Darkeye, "there are not worse people in that wicked country! They say that the old woman is a witch of some kind. But whether she poisons travellers or drowns them, I know not. No doubt she is in league with Ralph the robber, and would have robbed you or kept you fast in some way or other till you were handed over to him. You were right, my prince, in all you did. The only way of being delivered from temptation is to be brave, and do what is right, come what may." Then, grasping Eric by the hand, he led him back to the cottage. There Darkeye's wife received him like a mother, and all the children gathered round him in surprise and admiration, he looked so brave and lovely.

One of the walls of the cottage was reared on the edge of the rock, so that it seemed a continuation of it, and to rise up from the deep waters of the lake. The boys were thus able often to fish with a long line out of the window. A winding-stair led to a look-out on the roof, from which the whole island, called "The Green Island of the Lake," could be seen. It was about a mile or more in circumference, and was dotted all over with the cottages of the other foresters and king's huntsmen, each surrounded with clumps of trees, through which the curling smoke from the chimneys might be seen ascending. There were everywhere beautifully-kept gardens, with fruits, and flowers, and bee-hives; and fields, too, with their crops. On the green knolls and in the little valleys might be seen cows and sheep; while flocks of goats browsed among ivy-covered rocks. In the middle of the island was a little shallow lake, beside which the otter had his house among the rocks; and there the eagle also lived.

All the children in the island were the best of friends, and they played together, and sailed their boats on the little lake, and every day met in the house of one of the foresters to learn their lessons; and on Sunday, as they were very far away from any church, old Darkeye used to read the Good Book to them, and worship with them, and did all he could to make them love God and one another. There was also in the island a house, where, by the king's orders, all poor travellers could find refuge and refreshment. And it was a great pleasure to the boys and girls to visit them; and if they were sick and confined to bed, to attend to their wants. If the stranger had any children, the young islanders always shared their sports with them. And nothing pleased these stranger children more than to get leave to sail a boat, or to have the loan of a fishing-rod, or to hear the boys call Oscar, for that was the name of the otter, out of his den, and to play with Tor the eagle; or to see them feed Oscar with some of the fish they had caught, and Tor with a bit of meat. The dogs were so friendly, too, that they never touched Oscar, but would swim about in the same pool with him. And so all were happy in the Green Island; because Darkeye had taught them what a wicked thing selfishness was, and that the only way to be happy was by thinking about others as well as themselves, and by becoming like Him, the Elder Brother of us all, who "pleased not Himself." He also used to say:

"Now, when you work, work like men, and when you play, play like boys: be hearty at both." And so, while there was no idleness, there was abundance of recreation. Another evil was never permitted on the island, and that was, disobedience to parents, or want of respect to the old. But, indeed, punishment for these offences was seldom needed. The young learned to like to do what was right, and were too brave and manly to give pain and trouble to others, by forcing them to find fault or to punish. I should have mentioned, also, that they had a little band of musicians. One beat the drum, a few played the fife, and others some simple instrument; while almost all could sing tolerably well in parts. Thus, many a traveller would pause and listen with delight, as he heard, on a summer's evening, the chorus sung from many voices, or the music from the band coming from the island.

"Young people," Darkeye used to say, "have much wealth and happiness given them, for themselves and others, if they only used their gifts."

But I am forgetting Eric and Wolf. They were both, you may be sure, ready for their dinner, and there was laid for them on a table, cream, cakes, and fresh trout, and such other good things as the kind woman could get ready.

But now the thread began to move, as if it wished Eric to move also. Before rising to depart, he told Wolf how Darkeye, for his sake, would be so glad to take care of him, until he got his father's permission to bring him into the castle; that he would learn to be a huntsman, and be taught what was good, and to know about the Voice that spoke in his heart; and that all the boys in the island would make him their friend if he did what was right.

"Ralph will come here!" said Wolf, hanging his head.

"I wish the rascal did," said Darkeye, "for he would never go back. But he cannot enter my fort, and knows me and my huntsmen too well ever to try it. I have had more than one brush with the villain, and we hope soon to drive him and his brood from their bloody nest. Wolf, you are welcome and safe, for Eric's sake!" Then turning to Eric, he said, "I shall teach him, and make a man of him, my young prince, depend upon it. And now, before we part, I have to ask a favour," continued Darkeye. "You know our custom near evening? If the thread permits, remain, and be one of us." "I remember it," said Eric, "and will remain and be one of you, and let poor Wolf also be one."

And so they entered the cottage, and all sat down round an open window which looked out upon the beautiful lake with its wooded islands, and surrounded by the noble forest, above which rose the giant peaks and precipices. The water was calm as glass, and reflected every brilliant colour from rock and tree, and, most of all, from the golden clouds, which already began to gather in the west. Darkeye read from the Good Book of one who had left his father's house, and went to a far country, where he would fain have satisfied his hunger from the husks which the swine did eat, and could not, but who at last returned home after having suffered from his disobedience. When he closed the book, all stood up and sung these words with sweet and happy voices:--

"Father! from Thy throne above,
Bless our lowly home below!
Jesus, Shepherd! in Thy love,
Guard Thy flock from every foe.

"Thine we are! for Thou hast made us;
Thine, for we're redeem'd by Thee;
Thine, for Thou hast ever led us,
Thine, we evermore shall be!

"May we love Thee, may we fear Thee,
May Thy will, not ours, be done,
Never leave us till we're near
Thee In the Home where all are one!"

Then they knelt down, and Darkeye spoke to God in name of them all, thanking Him for His goodness, and telling Him their wants. When they rose from their knees, the gold thread shone brilliantly, and, like a beam of light, passed out at the door in the direction of the ferry.

During the singing of the verses, Wolf seemed for the first time quite overcome. He bent his head, and covered his face with his hands. He then said, in a low voice, when the short service was over, and as if speaking to himself, while all were silent listening to him,

"I had a dream. Long, long ago. A carriage--a lady. She was on her knees, with her hands clasped, and speaking to the sky. She had hold of me. Ralph was there and the robbers. I forget the rest."

He rose and looked out of the window, gazing vacantly.

"What can he mean?" asked Eric aside to Darkeye, who was looking tenderly on Wolf.

"Ah! who knows, poor boy! Singing always touches the heart of these wanderers. Perhaps--yes-- it may be," he said, so that Eric alone could hear him, "that he has been taken when a child by Ralph from some rich traveller, and perhaps his mother was killed! He may have been the child of good people. Was that person his mother who, he says, prayed for him? If so, her prayers are now answered, for her boy will be delivered,--poor Wolf!

"Wolf, my boy," said Darkeye, "come and bid farewell to your friend."

Wolf started as from a dream, and came to Eric.

"Farewell, my kind Wolf, and I hope to see you some day in my father's house." The herd spoke not a word, but wiped his eyes with the back of his rough hand. "Cheer up, Wolf, for you will be good and happy here."

"Wolf is happy already, and he will take care of the pigs, or do anything for you all."

He then held out his stick to Eric, and said, "Take it; keep it for my sake; it is all Wolf has to give;

Ralph has the gold coin."

"Thank you, good Wolf; but you will require it, and I need nothing to remember you."

"Don't be angry, Eric, for what I did to you in the forest when we first met. My heart is sorry."

"We did not know one another then, Wolf, and I shall never forget that it is to you I owe my escape."

"Wolf loves you, and every one here."

"I am sure you do, Wolf, and I love you. God bless you, Wolf, I must go; farewell!"

And thus they parted. But all gathered round Eric, and accompanied him to the boat, blessing the little prince, and wishing him a peaceful and happy journey. Eric thanked them with many smiles and tender words. Darkeye alone went with him into the boat, wondering greatly at the thread, and most of all at the prince, who shone with a beauty that seemed not of this world. The prince landed, but Darkeye knew, for many reasons, that he could not accompany him in his journey, which he must take alone. Eric embraced Darkeye, and waving his hand to all on the island, he was soon lost to their sight in the great forest.

A winding pathway, over the ridge of hills, led down to a broad and rapid but smooth river, and on its banks was a royal boat, splendid and rich to look upon. She was white as snow, with a purple seat at the end covered by a canopy, that gleamed with golden tassels and many gems. The thread led into the boat, and though no one was there, Eric entered, and sat on a purple cushion, on which the Gold Thread also laid itself down. No sooner had he gone on board of the boat, than--as if his little foot, when it touched her, had sent her from the shore--she slowly moved into the centre of the channel, and was carried downwards by the current. On she swept on the bosom of that clear stream, between shores adorned with all that could delight the eye--rocks and trees and flowers, with here and there foaming waterfalls, from mountain rivulets which poured themselves into the great river. The woods were full of song, and birds with splendid plumage flashed amidst the foliage like rainbow hues amidst the clouds. Eric knew not whither he was being carried, but his heart was sunshine and peace. On and on he swept with the winding stream, until at last, darting under a dark archway of rock, and then emerging into light, the boat grounded on a shore of pure white sand, while the thread rose and led him to the land. No sooner had he stepped on shore and ascended the green bank, than he found himself at the end of a long broad avenue of splendid old trees, whose tops met overhead. The far-off end of the avenue was closed by a great marble staircase, which ascended to a magnificent castle. Wall rose above wall, and tower over tower. He saw grand flights of stairs, leading from one stately terrace to another, with marble statues, clear gushing fountains, and flower-gardens, and every kind of lovely tree. It was his father's castle at last! He ran on with breathless anxiety and joy. He soon reached a large gate, that seemed to be covered with glittering gold.

As he looked at it, he saw the thread tied to a golden knocker upon it, shaped like the old cross in the forest. Inscribed over the gate were the words,

"He that persevereth to the end shall be saved."

He seized the knocker, and the moment it fell, the thread broke and vanished like a flash of light. A crash of music was then heard. The door opened, and there, in the midst of a court paved with marble of purest white, and on a golden throne, sat Eric's father, surrounded by his brothers and sisters. The beautiful lady was there too, and many, many more to welcome Eric. His father clasped him to his heart, and said,

"My son was lost, but is found!"

While all crowded round Eric to bid him welcome, with his weary feet and torn dress, kept together by the golden band, a chorus was heard singing,--

"Home where the weary rest,

Home where the good are blest,

Home of the soul; Glorious the race when run,

Glorious the prize when won,

Glorious the goal!"

Then there rose a swell of many young voices singing,--

"Oh, be joyful, be joyful, let every voice sing!

Welcome, brothers, our brother, the son of the king;

His wanderings are past, to his father he's come;

Little Eric, our darling, we welcome thee home!

"Oh, bless'd is the true one who follows the road,

Holding fast to his GOLD THREAD OF DUTY TO GOD,

Who, when tempted, is firm, who in danger is brave,

Who, forgetting himself, will a lost brother save.

Then be joyful, be joyful, for Eric is come;

Little Eric, our darling, we welcome thee home!"

And then the sun set, and the earth was dark, but the palace of the king shone like an aurora in the wintry sky.

The End

Here is a free preview of a Similar Title available From EirenikosPress

The Giant Killer
By
Charlotte Maria Tucker

1 THE GIANT KILLER

"Well, I hope that we're near the end of our journey at last!" exclaimed Adolphus Probyn, with a long weary yawn, as the fly which was conveying him and his brother from the station rolled slowly along a quiet county road.

"You're in a precious hurry to get there," said Constantine, fixing his thumbs in his waistcoat pockets, and putting up his feet on the opposite seat; " but I don't believe that you'll like the place when you see it. I hate being sent to a private tutor's; I'd rather have gone to a regular school at once."

"I don't know as to that," said Adolphus, who had some vague ideas in his mind about facing, hard dumplings, and wooden benches.

"One thing I know," cried his brother, "I'm certain to dislike this tutor with all my heart"

Adolphus did not take the trouble to ask his reasons, but Constantine went on without stopping to be questioned.

"I should dislike any one recommended by Aunt Lawrence she's so particular, thinks so many things wrong, is so fond of good books and lectures, and that sort of thing. Depend upon it, she put into papa's head that we were spoilt, and needed some one to keep us in order, and she found out this poor country clergyman"—

"Poor—I'm sorry he's poor," observed Adolphus; "he'll not make us half so comfortable as we were at home. I wonder if he'll have no late second dinner."

"Oh, you may make up your mind to that!" cried his brother; "all the family will dine together at One on boiled mutton and rice pudding, or bacon and beans!" Adolphus sighed. "And it will be work, work, work, from morning till night, with no change but long sermons, long lectures, and long walks; and if we go bird-nesting, or have a little fun, won't we catch it— that's all!"

"Here we are at last!" said Adolphus, as the fly stopped at a little green door.

THE FINISH OF THE JOURNEY.

Constantine put his head out of the window. "No carriage drive," he muttered; "what a mean place it must be!"

Scarcely had the coachman's pull at the bell broken the peaceful stillness of that quiet spot, when the green door was thrown wide open, and a boy of about eleven years of age appeared at it with a broad smile of welcome on his face.

"I'm so glad you've come—we've been waiting dinner for you; let me help down with that," he added, as the coachman made preparations for lifting down a black trunk which had kept him company on the box.

Constantine jumped from the carriage; his twin brother more slowly descended, and without troubling themselves with their luggage, or taking much notice of their new companion, they proceeded along the narrow gravel-walk which led up to the entrance of the dwelling.

A pretty cottage it appeared, though a small one, with the sunshine gleaming through the twining roses on the diamond-paneled windows that peeped from beneath the low thatched roof. It would have looked very well in a picture; not a chimney but was twisted into some elegant shape; the whole building, nestling in trees and garlanded with creepers, might have served as a model to a painter. But as Adolphus gazed curiously upon his new home, it looked to his eye rather too much like a magnified toy: he began to wonder to himself where room could be found in it for him and his brother, especially when he saw two little girls standing in the porch watching their arrival with a look of shy pleasure.

Boys of ten years of age are, however, seldom long troubled with thoughts such as these, and the attention of young Probyn was almost immediately diverted by the appearance of Mr. and Mrs. Roby, who advanced to welcome their guests to Dove's Nest. The former was a tall, pale gentleman, with a stoop, a high forehead and thoughtful air, which at once impressed the two little boys with an idea that a very learned scholar was before them. Mrs. Roby, on the contrary, was stout and rather short, with a bright merry glance in her dark eyes, to which the dimples in her cheeks corresponded; there was kindliness in the press of her hand, and a cheerful animation about her whole manner that made her guests feel at home with her at once.

THE RECEPTION.

"I see that my Aleck has introduced himself to you already," said she, smiling, "but here are other little friends glad to see you, and anxious, I am sure, to make you happy. Bertha—Laura—my darling," she continued, laying her hand fondly on the curly head of the youngest child, the little image of herself with her bright eyes and merry glance, "you should bid these young gentlemen welcome."

The Probyns were soon shown to the room which they were to share with Aleck; and though the ceiling was low, and sloped down on one side, and the single window was certainly small, he would have been difficult to please indeed, who could have found fault with so pretty an apartment. Everything was so beautifully clean and neat, and through that open window came so sweet an air; while the tinkle of a distant sheep-bell, and the carol of birds from the neighbouring trees, made music delightful, after the rattle of a railway, or the ceaseless roll of carriages in London.

The dinner, also, to which the Probyns speedily descended, was excellent, though simple; and Adolphus especially, who had soon managed to find out that no second one was to be expected, did ample justice to the good cheer after his long journey, having quite forgotten sundry parcels of sandwiches and cake which he had managed to dispose of by the way.

Being rather shy at first, and under the eye of Mr. Roby, the boys were upon their good behaviour, and everything went on very harmoniously. Laura had indeed to squeeze up very close to her mother to avoid the elbows of Constantine, and opened her merry eyes wider than usual when Adolphus, seeing that the plum-tart was rapidly disappearing, thrust forward his plate for a second help before he had half finished his first But no open notice was taken of either breach of good manners; this was not the time to find fault.

Mr. Roby sat quiet and observant, and his two little daughters said little; but their mother led the conversation, in which Aleck joined freely, and before the dinner was over the Probyns were quite at their ease.

"We shall have plenty of things to show you," said Aleck; "papa has given us all a half-holiday in honour of your arrival There are my two rabbits, the black and the white one."

"I like rabbit curry very much," interrupted Adolphus.

"Oh, but you are not to eat them!" exclaimed little Laura in alarm, shocked at the idea of cooking her favourites.

"And there is the garden," continued Aleck; "we have made two arches across the gravel-walk, and such beautiful creepers are twined round them; and there is a famous bower at the end of it—we helped to pave it with pebbles ourselves."

"And there's a cow!" cried Laura; "you shall see her milked!"

"Then we will have some syllabub, that we will!" exclaimed Adolphus.

The little Robys looked at each other, and then glanced at their mother, in astonishment at such a bold and unusual proposal. The lady, somewhat to their surprise, gave a smiling consent, and poured out nearly a tumbler-full of home-made wine in preparation for this unwonted treat.

"This is not so bad," thought Constantine; "I dare say we'' have some fun here. I shall like to tease that prim puss Miss Bertha a little, who looks as though she considered it wrong to open her mouth; and we'll bring down

Master Aleck a peg or two—he thinks himself mighty clever, I can see."

"This is a great deal better than school,"—such were the reflections of Adolphus. "The master looks mild enough, the lady is the picture of good-nature, and these people don't appear to be shabby, although they are certainly poor."

Yes, Mr. Roby was poor; even had his income been double what it was, one so generous and benevolent would still have been poor. He could not afford to give Aleck, his only son, the advantage of a school, but this seemed no misfortune to the affectionate father; he preferred conducting his boy's education himself. Aleck was naturally clever, and, under the careful training of his parent, had made uncommon progress in his studies. If there was anything on earth of which the clergyman was proud, it was the talents and goodness of his son. Quiet and reserved as Mr. Roby was, it was no small trial to him to introduce strangers into his peaceful home, though these strangers were the nephews of an intimate friend; it was a sacrifice of inclination to duty. But his wife, in encouraging him to make this sacrifice, had other reasons beyond increasing their small means, or obliging the aunt of the Probyns. Mrs. Roby, with her clear common sense, saw that it was not good for her Aleck to have no companion but his sisters. They were both younger than himself, and looked up to him in everything. He helped them in their lessons, took the lead in their amusements, and was loved by them with the fondest affection.

What wonder if the boy was becoming a little spoiled; he was of too much importance in the quiet home-circle; he could not but feel that his parents were proud of him—that his sisters regarded him as one who could scarcely do wrong; he grew too fond of giving his opinion—too self-confident, and his mother saw it. Hers was, however, the eye of partial affection, and she had little idea how often those who had been gratifying her husband by praising the uncommon talents and virtues of their son, behind his back spoke of him as "a conceited boy, who loved to hear himself talk, who was ruined by being brought up at home, and would never be good for anything in the world."

HELPING AT LESSONS.

Oh, how startled should we often be, could we know the difference between what is said to us, and what is said of us; what a shock would our vanity receive, could we look beyond the smile of flatterers and see into their hearts!

2 FIRST IMPRESSIONS

The next morning Aleck and his sisters met their mother in the breakfast-parlour before their guests had left their sleeping apartment. Mr. Roby was still engaged in his study, having as usual risen at five, that he might not leave one of his various duties neglected.

"Mamma," said Bertha, after having received her morning's kiss, "I am afraid that we shall not like these Probyns at all."

"It is too early to decide upon their characters," replied Mrs. Roby; "we must wait till we know them a little better."

"I think Constantine a very disagreeable boy," said Bertha; "he has a sort of—I don't know what sort of manner, but it is not in the least like Aleck's. It is as though he despised us for being girls; and he kicks his feet against the legs of the table, and never keeps still for a moment, and it fidgets me so—I can't bear it!" The little girl's brow was all wrinkled over with frowns.

"And he's so naughty," said Laura, resting her arms on her mother's knee, and looking up gravely into her face. "He pulled the cow's tail, and would not leave off, and when we told him that it hurt her, he only laughed!"

"You should have seen how the boys quarreled for the syllabub," continued Bertha, " pulling and struggling till half of it was thrown over between them."

"And they never let me have one drop," added Laura; "I think that they are shocking bad boys!"

"So they are," said Aleck, as he paused in his task of cutting the loaf for breakfast; "they never read their Bibles before going to bed, nor said their prayers neither, as far as I could tell." Aleck did not add—indeed, he did not consider, that although he himself had not omitted to kneel down, as he had been taught from his childhood to do, his thoughts had been so much taken up with his new companions, and drawing a contrast between their conduct and his own, that not a feeling of real devotion had given life to his heartless prayer.

"Not say their prayers!" cried Laura, looking more shocked than before; "did you ever think that there were such wicked boys?"

"And such stupid ones too," rejoined Aleck. " When I spoke to them about their lessons, Adolphus said, with a great yawn, that learning was a bore." Laura raised her eyebrows with an expression of arch surprise. "

"I offered to lend him my account of the famous Cook. 'Oh, I know all about him already', said he; 'his name was Soyer, and he made a capital sauce'!" Here two merry dimples appeared on the little child's cheeks, and deepened as her brother proceeded: "And when I asked him if he did not like Caesar, he thought that I was speaking of a dog, and inquired if he was one that would not bite!"

This overcame Laura's gravity altogether; she burst into such a merry ringing laugh that neither Bertha nor Aleck could help joining her heartily; and even Mrs. Roby, who was meditating a little lecture to her children on too hastily judging others, found it difficult to keep her countenance.

The entrance of the Probyns stopped the mirth of which they had been the subject. Breakfast passed over; then came hours of study, which served to strengthen Aleck in his opinion that his companions were very stupid boys. Adolphus appeared the dullest of the two; not that he naturally was so, but he had always been too lazy to learn. He stumbled at every word in his reading, spelt pheasant with an f, and thumb without a b, could not see any difference between a noun and a verb, and confused the Red Sea with the Black. Poor Mr. Roby, accustomed to an intelligent pupil, stifled a quiet sigh; and Aleck, with a feeling of vast superiority, could not hide the mingled surprise, amusement, and contempt, which the boy's ignorance called up in his own mind. The Probyns noticed the smile on his face, and it stung them more than a real injury would have done; while indulging his secret pride, Aleck was sowing in the hearts of his companions bitter feelings of resentment and hate.

After lessons, an hour was given to play in the garden; but anything but play it proved to Aleck, for the Probyns were determined to show him that, if he had more book-learning than they, he, a country boy, was ignorant of many things familiar to them from living in London. Without coming to an open quarrel, they made him feel that they disliked him, showed such open contempt for what he valued, and treated his favourite pursuits with such scorn, that, irritated almost beyond his power of endurance by a trial to which he was unaccustomed, Aleck lost both his patience and his temper, and was laughed at for being so easily "put in a pet." It was fortunate for him that the time had now come for joining his mother and sisters in the parlour. The boys found the little ladies busy at their sewing; Mrs. Roby had quitted the room to see a poor woman who had come for advice and assistance.

"This is our nice half-hour with mamma," said Laura; "she always reads something to us before dinner while we work, and Aleck draws beside her."

"More reading!" exclaimed Adolphus, with no pleased look.

"Oh, but it's amusing reading!" said Laura. "There, Aleck dear, I've put your copy and pencil all ready for you; and I've not forgotten the India - rubber this morning, you see, though I am such a careless little thing!" Another time she would have been repaid by a smile and a kiss; but Aleck was in no mood for that now.

"Amusing reading! I wonder what you call amusing!" said Constantine, who, to Bertha's great annoyance, was occupying his idle fingers in turning over the contents of her work-box.

"Why, mamma has been reading to us little bits," said Laura; "only little bits such as I can understand, you know, of the history of good Mr. Budgett, the "Successful Merchant.""

"The Successful Merchant! I'll not stand that!" exclaimed Constantine, flinging Bertha's reels of cotton right and left, as he threw himself back in his chair.

"Oh, but it's so curious—so interesting—and all true! There's the story of the little donkey, and of the horse that was lost, and the great tea-party—things that amuse even me."

"Amuse a stupid girl like you; but"—

"If you talk about stupidity," cried Aleck, firing up, "let me tell you "—

Oh, how thankful the girls were for the entrance of their mother at this moment. To see flushed faces, fiery looks, clenched fists, was so new to them, that, in terror lest their darling brother should be drawn into a quarrel and be hurt, poor little Laura could scarcely restrain her tears, and Bertha, as she stooped to pick up her reels, wished from her heart that these odious new-comers had never arrived to break the peaceful serenity of Dove's Nest.

Mrs. Roby's quick eye instantly detected that there had been words amongst the children; she thought it best, however, to take no notice of this, and opening a little drawer in her table, took out of it a manuscript book.

"I have been thinking what kind of reading might serve to entertain you all, uniting some instruction with amusement." Constantine turned down his lips at the word instruction. He thought that the lady did not see him. "Here is an allegory—a sort of tale which contains a hidden meaning beneath the apparent one— and"—

"But I don't like hearing reading, ma'am," interrupted Adolphus, with much more candour than good manners.

"No kind of reading?" inquired Mrs. Roby, in perfect good-humour.

"Oh, some story-books, and fairy-tales, I don't mind them, if I've nothing better to amuse me."

"I think, then, that this book may suit your taste; it is the story of a Giant-killer."

"Jack the Giant-killer I Oh, I've heard that a thousand times!" cried Adolphus, while Robyn could scarcely help laughing at the idea of their mother reading such a story to them.

"Mine is a new Giant-killer—a great hero, I can assure you," said the lady; " and I think that my tale is a better one than that with which you are so well acquainted, as it contains a great deal that is true." "Why, there are no giants now!" cried Conatantine, "I am not so sure of that," replied Mrs. Roby; "I believe that we might find both giants and giant-killers in the world at this time, if we only knew where to look for them."

"I should like to hear this story," said Constantine, afraid of the lady's returning to the "Successful Merchant."

"Then perhaps you would kindly wind this skein of silk for me while I read," said Mrs. Roby, willing to save an unfortunate tidy from the fingers which were now picking at its fringe. "There, let me find the end for you. I am sure that Adolphus will oblige me by turning the skein while you wind; and, now that you are all busily employed, I will at once begin my little book."

WINDING THE SKEIN.

3 GIANT SLOTH

It was the still hour of twilight. The moon still shone in the deep blue sky; but her light was becoming pale and dim. The stars had gone out, one by one, and a red flush in the east, deepening into crimson just behind the hill, showed where the sun would shortly appear.

A knight lay stretched on the mossy ground ; his head reclined on a shield, his two-handed sword girt to his side—even in sleep his hand rested on the hilt. This was the brave champion Fides, the chosen knight to whom had been given mighty treasures and a golden crown by the King whom he had served from his childhood. But he was not yet to enter into possession of his riches, he was not yet to wear his bright crown; hard labours, great dangers were before him—he was to fight before he might enjoy. So Fides was to pass alone through the enemy's land, to slay every giant who should oppose him on the way. His King had provided him with strong armour, and with a wondrous sword which gave certain victory if he who drew it shrank not back like a coward, or yielded to the foe like a traitor; he had, in truth, nothing to fear but his own slackness in fight; if but faithful, he must be triumphant.

The knight slept soundly on his soft couch, for he was weary with long travel that night. He was roused by the touch of a hand, so light that the dew could hardly have rested more gently on his shoulder; and yet there was something in the power of that touch which not only broke his slumbers, but restored to him in a moment all his waking powers. He started up, and beheld before him a beautiful messenger sent by his King. Her robe was of woven light, a starry crown was upon her head, and the glance of her eye penetrated the heart, and laid open its most inmost feelings. Fides recognized Conscience, his companion and friend, who, invisible to all eyes but his own, had come on an errand to the knight.

"Sleeping still!" she exclaimed, "with your labours all to come—sleeping on the enemy's ground! Rouse you, recreant champion, and draw your sword; see you not yon towers before you? It is there that Giant Sloth holds his court; you cannot pass on until he is slain. This is the hour to attack him in his hold; soon after sunrise he quits it to roam abroad; if not attacked early, he will escape your pursuit;—on, then, and victory attend you!"

KNIGHT FIDES AND CONSCIENCE.

"O Conscience, I am weary!" Fides replied; "a little more rest may be mine! The sun is scarcely seen above yon ridge; grant me another hour's slumber," "Go at once," replied the bright one, "or you go in vain"

"But how make my way into the castle?" "Press the hilt of your sword against the heaviest door, and it will open as if by a key."

"But if difficulties should arise, or doubts perplex me."

"Breathe upon the hilt of your sword, and you will behold me beside you. Though unseen, I will ever be near you. Delay not now, for, look at the sun, what a flood of light he pours on the world! When the great clock in the giant's tower strikes six, it will be too late to encounter him that day; he may vanish before your eyes, but neither be conquered nor slain. Go!" And even as the words were upon her lips, the bright one vanished from his sight.

With rapid step and a resolute spirit. Fides sped on to his first encounter. The way was plain before him; not even the youngest child could have mistaken it. In front arose the castle of Giant Sloth, whose heavy, shapeless mass looked as though it had been built of clouds. Fides, sword in hand, pressed up to the door; it was open, as if to invite his entrance, and he at once proceeded into the large hall.

A strange scene of confusion was there; the whole place was littered with unfinished work, blotted pages and blank ones, play-books torn and without their backs, dresses in rags, and neglected volumes with leaves yet uncut. But the strangest thing was the feeling of heaviness and dullness which stole over the knight the moment that he entered the hall. It seemed too much trouble even to pass through its length; he would fain have laid himself down and slept. The place was very still, the only sound heard was that of some one heavily breathing in a room that was near; Fides doubted not that this was the giant himself.

Animated with the hope of gaining his first triumph, the knight resolutely struggled against the sleepy sensation which made the danger of that enchanted hall. He passed through it, and found at the end that what he at a distance had mistaken for a wall, was only a huge web, like that which the house-spider weaves; not the light net-work which is strung with bright beads of dew, but thick, close, and darkened with dust. Through this strange curtain Fides with some difficulty could see into the inner room where the giant lay asleep.

Sloth's huge, clumsy form was half sunk in a great heap of down, not a feather of which stirred in the heavy air, except such as were moved by his breathing. Here, then, was the knight, and there was his foe, but how was the first to reach the latter! Only the web was between, and Fides threw his whole weight against it, hoping easily thus to get through; not so, it bent, but it did not break—every thread in the yielding curtain seemed as strong as though it had been made of iron wire.

Fides drew back disappointed and surprised; something that was not weariness, but possessed the same power to deaden energy and make effort disagreeable, seemed pressing his spirit down. His eyelids grew heavy, he could scarcely keep them open, he felt a strong and increasing desire to indulge the sleepiness which had now come over him. But there was an object before him which made him struggle against the enchantment. Just above the feathery couch of the giant was a huge clock, with a dial of silver and numbers of gold, and the hand, which glittered with many a gem, had almost touched the point of six.

"Now or never!" thought Fides, with another strong effort, as he remembered the words of Conscience. Again the web yielded to his weight, but not the smallest flaw appeared in its fine texture to give him hope of succeeding in breaking through.

"Ding—ding—ding !" the hand is at six—the giant is beginning to stir! Fides with sudden resolution lifts his sword on high, down it descends on the web, which, as the blow divides it, starts back on each side till a very wide gap appears. Fides springs through the opening, he is just in time, and the next moment Giant Sloth lies dead at his feet.

FIDES SLAYS THE GIANT SLOTH.

"Well," exclaimed Adolphus, with a comical expression on his face, as soon as Mrs. Roby had closed her book, "I suspect that this story, from beginning to end, is all a hit upon me."

"I thought that it was a hit upon me," said little Laura, "when I heard of the broken-backed play-books, and the room in such shocking disorder!"

"It might have been a hit upon me," thought Bertha, who, indolent by disposition, had felt the moral touch her in the description of unfinished work.

"It is a hit upon no one," replied Mrs. Roby, "unless any person present chooses to consider himself as Giant Sloth or one of his brotherhood. Your faults are your enemies, the greatest enemies of those over whom they exercise the greatest power. Pray, at this our first reading of "the Giant-killer," let me impress this strongly upon your minds. I would not hurt the feelings of one of my listeners, far less would I encourage them to find out and laugh at the follies of each other. My desire is to lead you to consider that you are all and each of you yourselves in the position of my hero. The foes which he had to conquer you also must fight; you have the same aid to encourage you, the same motives to rouse. The same giant may not be equally formidable to you all, but every one has some enemy with whom he must struggle, in a strength that is given to him, armour not his own."

"Ah!" said Aleck, "I was sure that there was some meaning in that part of the story. The two-handed sword also, which nothing could resist"—

"What was that?" interrupted Constantine.

"I would rather that you should discover that for yourself," said Mrs. Roby. " If the kernel of an allegory be good, it is worth the trouble of cracking the shell"

"Oh, but I hate all trouble!" cried Adolphus; "above all, the trouble of thinking."

" Take care, take care," laughed little Laura, "or we shall suspect that you have been caught by Giant Sloth."

The rest of this book is available to purchase through Amazon.com in ebook or paperback format. Search for EirenikosPress to find this and many more great titles.

Made in the USA
Coppell, TX
09 January 2024